OTHER BOOKS BY JEFF KINNEY

Diary of a Wimpy Kid

Diary of a Wimpy Kid: Rodrick Rules

Diary of a Wimpy Kid: The Last Straw

Diary of a Wimpy Kid: Dog Days

Diary of a Wimpy Kid Do-It-Yourself Book

The Wimpy Kid Movie Diary

COMING SOON

More *Diary of a Wimpy Kid*

DIARY
of a
Wimpy Kid
THE UGLY TRUTH

by Jeff Kinney

PUFFIN BOOKS

PUFFIN BOOKS

Published by the Penguin Group
Penguin Group (Australia)
250 Camberwell Road, Camberwell, Victoria 3124, Australia
(a division of Pearson Australia Group Pty Ltd)
Penguin Group (USA) Inc.
375 Hudson Street, New York, New York 10014, USA
Penguin Group (Canada)
90 Eglinton Avenue East, Suite 700, Toronto, Canada ON M4P 2Y3
(a division of Pearson Penguin Canada Inc.)
Penguin Books Ltd
80 Strand, London WC2R 0RL England
Penguin Ireland
25 St Stephen's Green, Dublin 2, Ireland
(a division of Penguin Books Ltd)
Penguin Books India Pvt Ltd
11 Community Centre, Panchsheel Park, New Delhi – 110 017, India
Penguin Group (NZ)
67 Apollo Drive, Rosedale, North Shore 0632, New Zealand
(a division of Pearson New Zealand Ltd)
Penguin Books (South Africa) (Pty) Ltd
24 Sturdee Avenue, Rosebank, Johannesburg 2196, South Africa

Penguin Books Ltd, Registered Offices: 80 Strand, London, WC2R 0RL, England

First published in 2010 by Amulet Books (USA), an imprint of ABRAMS
First published by Penguin Books (Australia), 2010

5 7 9 10 8 6 4

Book design by Jeff Kinney
Cover design by Chad W. Beckerman and Jeff Kinney
Printed and bound in Australia by McPherson's Printing Group, Maryborough, Victoria

National Library of Australia
Cataloguing-in-Publication data:

Kinney, Jeff.
Wimpy kid : the ugly truth / Jeff Kinney.

ISBN 978 0 14 330499 9 (pbk.)

813.6

puffin.com.au

TO TOMAS

SEPTEMBER

Thursday

It's been almost two and a half weeks since me and my ex-best friend, Rowley Jefferson, had our big fight. To be honest with you, I thought he would've come crawling back to me by now, but for some reason, that hasn't happened.

I'm actually starting to get a little concerned, because school starts back up in a few days, and if we're gonna get this friendship back on track, something needs to happen quick. If me and Rowley really ARE through, that would stink, because the two of us had a pretty good thing going.

Now that our friendship is history, I'm in the market for a new best friend. The problem is, I invested all my time in Rowley, and I don't have anyone lined up to take his place.

The two best options I have at this point are Christopher Brownfield and Tyson Sanders. But each of those guys has his own issues.

CHRISTOPHER   TYSON

I hung out with Christopher for the last few weeks of the summer, mostly because he's a really excellent mosquito magnet. But Christopher is more of a summertime friend than a school-year friend.

Tyson is nice enough, and we like the same video games. But he pulls his pants all the way down when he uses the urinal, and I don't know if I can ever get past that.

The only other kid my age who's not paired up with someone is Fregley, but I ruled him out as best friend material a long time ago.

Anyway, I'm still keeping the door open a crack for Rowley, just in case. But if he wants to save this friendship, he'd better do something fast.

Because the way things stand, he's not gonna come out looking very good in my autobiography.

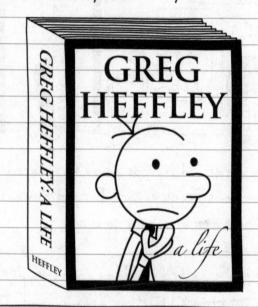

CHAPTER 8
CHILDHOOD

I used to live near this kid. I think his name was Rupert or Roger or something.

With my luck, though, I'll go on to be rich and famous and Rowley will STILL find a way to ride my coat-tails.

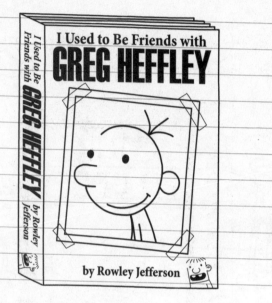

Saturday
The reason I don't see things changing between me and Rowley is because he's already found himself a replacement friend. Or to be more accurate, his PARENTS did.

For the past few weeks Rowley's been hanging out with this teenager named Brian.

Whenever I go by Rowley's house, he's out in his front yard throwing a football or a Frisbee with a guy who looks like he's in high school or college.

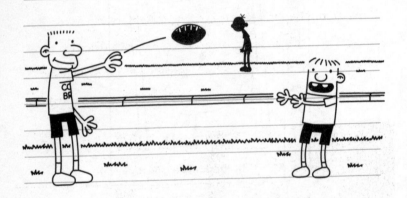

Well, I did some poking around and found out that this Brian guy isn't just some normal kid from the neighbourhood. He's part of a company called 'Cool Brian,' which is sort of like a big-brother-for-hire kind of thing.

In fact, I'd be willing to bet money this guy's name isn't even really Brian.

Mum said she thinks the Cool Brian thing is a great idea because it gives kids a 'role model' they can look up to. That makes me kind of mad because, the way I see it, I'M Rowley's role model.

And now Rowley's parents are paying some guy to do what I've been doing all these years for FREE.

The thing that really burns me is that Rowley probably doesn't even know his parents are paying this guy to spend time with him. And I don't think it would bother Rowley if he DID know the truth.

Today I saw Rowley hanging out with a different Cool Brian, so Rowley's regular guy must've had the day off. But I could tell Rowley didn't even notice.

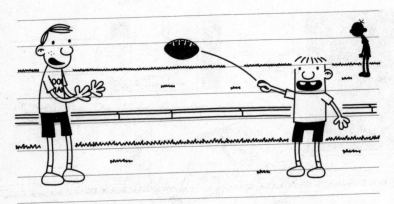

Tuesday
Today was the first day of school. I don't want to jinx things, but it's looking like this could be a great year for me.

In homeroom we got our textbooks for the semester. My school can't afford to get new books every year, so we usually get hand-me-downs.

But when you get a book that ten kids had before you, it makes it kind of hard to do any actual learning.

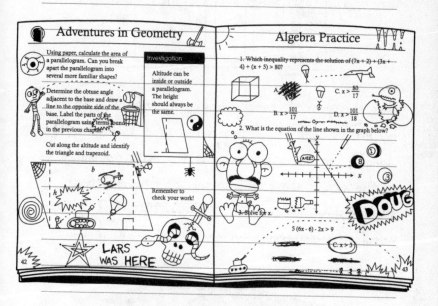

Usually, I have really bad luck when it comes to previous book owners. Last year I got a maths book that had belonged to Bryan Goot.

And that didn't exactly up my 'cool' factor in the hallways.

But this year I totally lucked in. When I got my maths book, I found out it used to belong to Jordan Jury. Jordan Jury is the most popular kid in the grade above me, so carrying his textbook around should translate into some MAJOR popularity points.

One reason Jordan is so popular is because he always has these big blowout parties, and it's really hard to get invited. But I figure this Algebra book could be just the thing I need to get on his radar.

Speaking of popular kids, I sat near Bryce Anderson and his group of friends at lunch today. Bryce is basically the Jordan Jury of my grade, and he's got a bunch of cronies who are always going along with everything he says.

And those guys are loyal to Bryce no matter how dumb he makes them look.

See, Bryce Anderson has the right idea. He doesn't actually NEED a best friend, because he's got a bunch of lackeys who basically worship him. The reason me and Rowley didn't make it is because we were equal partners in our friendship, and I don't think that kind of model has a chance of working out.

Friday
At school today I heard Rowley tell some kid he was going to a rock concert tonight. I admit I was a little jealous, since I've never been to a real concert myself. But when I found out who was performing, I was glad I wasn't invited.

Still, it kind of irks me that Rowley is having more fun than I am. In fact, it seems like EVERYONE is having more fun than me these days.

There are some kids in my grade who post their pictures online.

And from the looks of things, they're all having a WAY better time than I am.

I don't want people thinking MY life is lame, so I decided to take some pictures to show how great things are going for me.

All you really need is a digital camera and a photo-editing program and you can make it look like you're having a total blast.

Tonight I was right in the middle of creating a wild New Year's Eve party scene when I got busted by Mum.

Oh well. Mum won't let me post photos on the computer anyway, because of 'privacy' and all that. Or maybe it's because she learned her lesson after letting my older brother, Rodrick, post HIS pictures.

Rodrick's been trying to get a job so he can buy a new drum set, but nobody will hire him. Mum told him that nowadays employers look up the people they're thinking of hiring and that his pictures are probably hurting his chances.

So Rodrick replaced his band pictures with this one —

Wednesday

This year everyone in my grade has to take
Advanced Health, which covers some top-secret
stuff that I guess they didn't think we were
ready for until now.

In the first few classes, the boys and girls were
mixed together, but today Nurse Powell said she
was gonna split us up. She sent the girls down to
Mrs Gordon's room and then she put in a video for
us boys to watch.

From what I could tell, the video was at least thirty years old, so I'm sure Dad watched the same exact tape when he was my age.

I'm not gonna describe everything that they showed in the video, because it was actually pretty disgusting. If you ask me, some of that stuff doesn't really belong in a classroom.

Rowley didn't even make it through the whole video. He passed out at the two-minute mark when they said the word 'perspiration'.

To be honest with you, I don't know if Rowley's ready for this stuff. He's basically like a little kid. He told me once that he avoids the older kids at school because he's afraid he's gonna 'catch puberty'.

In fact, now that I think about it, I haven't seen Cool Brian for a while. So I wonder if Rowley's avoiding him, too, because he thinks he's contagious.

The same kind of thing happened in last year's
Health class when they did a smoking unit. The
teacher said that you never know who's going to
offer you a cigarette, and that it could even be
your best friend.

Well, after Rowley heard THAT, he wouldn't even
walk on the same side of the street as me for a
solid MONTH.

Believe me, I don't need some teacher to tell ME it's not cool to smoke. My grandfather convinced me of that last year on Thanksgiving.

Anyway, I think Rowley's just one of those kids who are always gonna be a few years behind everyone else maturity-wise. Rowley doesn't even know how to tie his shoes yet, because he's the kind of person who has Velcro everything.

RRRIP

Last year Rowley's Mum bought him sneakers with laces, and I can't even tell you how many times I had to bail him out.

I guess it probably should've been a warning sign that my best friend was impressed that I knew how to tie my own shoes.

Thursday
Today I was reading the comics in the newspaper, and I saw an ad that caught my attention.

It was for Peachy Breeze Ice-Cream, and apparently they're looking for a new spokesperson.

Peachy Breeze has those commercials on TV that run non-stop, with that kid with the freckles and the high-pitched voice.

The Peachy Breeze Kid used to be kind of cute, but over the years he's gotten a little seedy-looking.

So I guess they're looking for someone to take his place.

Well, I'd be PERFECT for the role. First of all, I LOVE ice-cream, so it wouldn't be hard for me to do the acting part. Second, I would be willing to miss a lot of school to fulfil my Peachy Breeze obligations.

And they wouldn't have to worry about me getting too old for the part, because I'd take whatever I needed to take to stop growing.

The only stumbling block I can see is that Dad HATES the Peachy Breeze TV ads because he thinks the kid is annoying. So I don't think he'd be too thrilled if I became their new spokesperson.

There's just something about that kid that gets on Dad's nerves. In fact, I think he hates the Peachy Breeze Kid even more than he hates Li'l Cutie, which is saying something.

Every time Dad sees a Peachy Breeze commercial on TV, he writes the Peachy Breeze people an angry letter saying that the ads drive him crazy and he'll never buy any of their products.

A few weeks later, Dad gets a response in the mail from Peachy Breeze, and it's always the same thing: coupons for free ice-cream.

It's been going on like this for years, and if something doesn't change, we're gonna have to get an extra freezer to hold all of our Peachy Breeze ice-cream.

Saturday
I told Mum about the Peachy Breeze Kid contest last night, and she said it seemed like an 'exciting opportunity'. But it turns out she was thinking of my little brother, Manny, when she said that.

In fact, this morning Mum and Manny were ready to take off for the audition without me, but I caught them just in time.

Mum seemed surprised that I wanted to be
the Peachy Breeze Kid and said I might be
'too old' for the part. At first I thought
that was ridiculous, but when I saw my
competition at the mall, I could kind of see
where she was coming from.

TRYOUTS

I figured I could charm the judges and get the
job anyway. Plus, I had an edge, because I was
the only kid trying out who could read a cue card.

There must've been two hundred kids in line, and
I realised that if I wanted the job, I was
gonna have to come up with some sort of gimmick.
So I decided I'd jump up and click my heels
together when I said the Peachy Breeze slogan.

But when it was finally my turn to go, things didn't work out the way I'd planned.

I knew my chances of getting the part weren't good when the casting people sent me out the door without even asking my name.

My opportunity was slipping away, so I did what I could to improve my odds.

But it looks like the job is gonna go to a younger kid after all, which really stinks.

You know, this isn't the first time I've been discriminated against because of my age, either. Last October me and Rowley heard that our local news station was going to be at the Red Apple Farm to shoot footage of kids carving pumpkins and making scarecrows and stuff like that.

We knew this was our big chance to be on TV, so we plopped ourselves in front of the news camera and really hammed it up.

But it took about five seconds for the news people to kick us out.

Then they brought in some little kids to take our place, and they did the same EXACT thing me and Rowley were doing.

And sure enough, those kids were on the news that night.

The truth is, this kind of thing has been going on for a long time. And where it's worst is in my own family.

Up until I was eight or nine, I was the star of every family gathering. It seemed like nobody could get enough of me.

But after Manny was born, things really changed for me.

See, when you're a little kid, nobody ever warns you that you've got an expiration date. One day you're hot stuff and the next day you're a dirt sandwich.

I guess I can understand why Rodrick's always so grumpy. It's been a long time since he was the centre of attention, and believe me, he's not getting any cuter.

The person who's lucky is ROWLEY. He's an only child, so at least he doesn't have to worry about being replaced by the next kid to come along.

Monday

Tonight at dinner Dad told us that his younger brother, Uncle Gary, got engaged to his girlfriend, Sonja. I guess that's great news and all, but Uncle Gary has been married three times before, so this has kind of become a regular thing in our family. In fact, we don't even use growth charts at home, because we can just look at pictures from Uncle Gary's weddings to keep track of our progress.

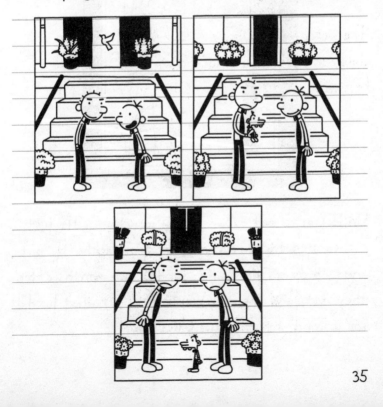

So I think everyone's a little burned out by now. When Uncle Gary got married the THIRD time, Mum didn't even bother to replace the picture of his second wedding on the mantel. She just taped a photo of the new wife's head on top of the old one.

Uncle Gary's not a bad guy or anything. He just rushes into these relationships too quickly. He got engaged to his first wife, Linda, two months after they met, and she didn't even find out what he did for a living until their wedding day.

And I heard Uncle Gary's second wife, Charlene, thought he had a lot of money because of a miscommunication on their second date.

It turns out Uncle Gary only had forty-five dollars, not forty-five THOUSAND dollars.

But Charlene didn't find that out until it was time to pay the band at the wedding.

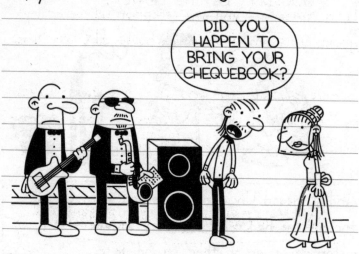

Dad's always saying Uncle Gary needs to 'grow up' and stop acting like a child. But if I were Dad, I wouldn't hold my breath.

Tuesday

I found out that Uncle Gary's wedding is gonna be in November, and the reception will be at my great-grandmother Gammie's house, like last time.

Gammie is ninety-five years old, but she still lives in the big house where she grew up. She's like the official head of the whole Heffley family.

Gammie is one of the only people in the world who still writes letters. And when she writes you a letter, she expects you to write one BACK.

I've tried to explain to Gammie that people my age don't know how to write letters with a stamp and a 'return address' and all that stuff, but she doesn't wanna hear it.

At Uncle Gary's last wedding, Gammie handed me a starter letter plus an envelope with her address and a stamp on it so I wouldn't have any excuse not to write.

G. HEFFLEY
12 SURREY STREET

GAMMIE HEFFLEY
38 BACON STREET
EAST W

Dear Gammie,

Love,
Gregory

But I STILL haven't filled it in and mailed it yet. So now every time I walk past my desk in my bedroom, I feel guilty.

Gammie is ALWAYS making you feel guilty. Last year at Thanksgiving, I put a whoopee cushion on her chair, and she sat on it.

A few days later everyone in the whole family got a handwritten apology letter from Gammie.

Dear Family,

I am writing to apologise for the unfortunate incident that occured shortly after our family concluded 'grace' at our Thanksgiving celebration. As I have gotten older, I have found it more difficult to control my body, and I'm afraid my recent surgery may have contributed to my little 'slip.'

I hope that this unfortunate mishap does not become the lasting impression of what was otherwise a glorious and blessed occasion.

Love,
Gammie

Sometimes I wonder if Gammie is just messing with everyone and does this kind of thing on purpose. Last Easter she invited the whole family to her house, but everyone had their own thing going on, and nobody went.

Gammie called Dad on Easter Sunday and said she'd bought a scratch ticket and won the ten-million-dollar grand prize. Word got around the family quick, and everyone was at Gammie's house in no time flat.

But it turned out the scratch ticket wasn't a winner after all.

YOU HAVE TO MATCH THREE OF THE FRUITS TO WIN, GAMMIE.

I SEE.

Gammie didn't seem too bothered that she wasn't a multimillionaire after all, and I have a feeling she got what she REALLY wanted anyway.

I hope I live to be ninety-five years old, because if I do, I guarantee you I'll be messing with people, too.

What makes me kind of nervous about going to Gammie's house in November is that it's time for me to get 'the Talk'. Every time someone in my family gets to be about my age, Gammie sits them down and talks to them about who-knows-what. I guess it's one of those elder-wisdom kinds of things.

The last person to get 'the Talk' from Gammie was Rodrick, and now I'm next in line. I'm hoping Uncle Gary breaks off his engagement so we don't have to go down there, because the whole thing is making me a nervous wreck.

Thursday
We've got a new maths teacher at our school named Mrs Mackelroy.

She used to teach kindergarten, and I don't think she's real crazy about middle school kids.

We have maths right after Phys Ed, so by the time we get to Mrs Mackelroy's room, everyone's all sweaty from exercising.

Mrs Mackelroy complained to the principal and said she can't teach when it smells like a 'monkey house' in the room, so the principal said that from now on us kids have to take showers after gym.

Well, I can tell you that most of the boys in my class were not on board with that decision.

The only person who was OK with it was Roger
Townsend, but he was held back twice and he's
practically a man anyway.

So the rest of us decided we were gonna have
to fake it. After Phys Ed was over yesterday,
we all took turns getting our hair wet so it
LOOKED like we showered.

I don't know if we really fooled Mrs Mackelroy, but I don't think she's ever gonna go into the boys' locker room and investigate.

This showering situation reminds me of something that happened over the summer, when me and Rowley were still friends. I used to go up to Rowley's house just about every day, but the problem was that I had to walk past Fregley's house each time.

I remembered Rodrick saying that a person could make it all the way from our house to the top of the hill by crawling through the drainage pipe.

I decided to see if he was right, and believe it or not, he was. It was pretty dark and nasty in that drainage pipe, but it was totally worth crawling through it to avoid Fregley.

When I headed back home, I went through the drainage pipe again.

But I probably should've hosed off in the front
yard or something, because Mum seemed suspicious
when I walked through the front door.

I knew Mum would have a fit if she found out I
crawled through the drainage pipe, so I didn't
say anything. But Mum told me I was gonna
have to take a shower before dinner. When I
got out of the bathroom, there was something
sitting on my bed.

I opened it up and found a stick of deodorant and a book.

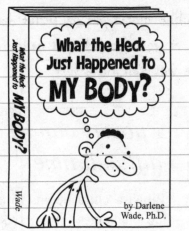

I put the deodorant on my dresser, but I tossed the book in the trash. I'd seen that one before. Mum must've gotten the same book for Rodrick when he was my age, and I found it in his junk drawer. And believe me, I do not need to see the pictures in that book a second time.

And what's worse is that Mum made me the subject of her parenting column in our local paper that week. She didn't use my actual name, but I don't think it would've taken a detective to figure out who she was talking about.

Puberty can be a difficult time

Susan Heffley

When a child begins to experience the changes that come with adolescence, the transformation can be uncomfortable, awkward, or even frightening. But given the right guidance, a child can learn to welcome, and even celebrate, the transition into adulthood. My second-born son recently began his wondrous journey into his new

Sunday

Tonight Mum called a 'house meeting'. And whenever she does that, it's never good. The last time we had a house meeting, it was so she could complain about the situation in the bathroom.

She said she was tired of having to clean the floor around the toilet because of our 'lousy aim'.

I knew exactly what she was talking about, too. One time I actually missed the bus because I used the bathroom after Manny.

GREG, YOU'RE GONNA MISS THE BUS!

I THINK I'M STUCK TO THE FLOOR!

All I can say is, I'm not the one causing the problem. When Rodrick uses the bathroom, half the time he doesn't even turn on the light.

Mum said the new rule was that us boys were gonna have to sit down every time we used the bathroom, no matter what.

But none of us guys liked THAT idea. Rodrick
suggested we just buy a couple of urinals, since
there are more of US than there are of HER.
Plus, that way, more than one person could go at
the same time.

But Mum said that would be 'tacky,' and she used
her veto power to shut his idea down.

I thought tonight's house meeting was gonna be
a follow-up to the bathroom meeting, since nobody
was following the sitting-down rule and things
are worse than ever. But this meeting was about
something completely different.

Mum told us that she was going back to study and that she was gonna start taking classes a few times a week.

Well, I was totally caught off guard by this news. Mum's ALWAYS there when I get home from school, and that's the way I like it.

But Mum said that after all these years of staying at home with us kids, she needs to do something that stimulates her mind. So she said she's gonna take classes for a semester and see how it goes.

I guess I can understand why Mum would want to branch out, because if I did the kinds of things she does every day, I'd probably be going bananas, too.

MUMMY & ME DANCE CLASS

Mum said us men are gonna have to make our own dinners a few nights a week and start doing chores that she usually takes care of herself.

One of those chores is making lunches, and to be honest with you, I'm pretty happy that one is getting turned over to us.

Mum writes a note on our lunch bags every day, and I can definitely live without THAT.

Dear Gregory—
Have a healthy, happy day!

Love,
Mum

Wednesday

OK, so the first few nights with Mum away have been a disaster. We tried making dinner on our own on Monday, but none of us knew what we were doing.

Manny was in charge of making the iced tea, but it was undrinkable since he stirred it with his bare hands.

STIR
STIR

Rodrick was in charge of cooking the roast beef, but he forgot to take the plastic wrap off before putting it in the oven.

So we bagged the homemade meal idea and went out to eat. When we left the restaurant, Rodrick spat his gum at some moths that were flying around, and he hit Dad by accident.

Dad chased Rodrick around the parking lot, but Rodrick is actually pretty fast, and Dad couldn't catch him. Then Dad tripped over a curb and twisted his ankle.

So Rodrick had to drive Dad to the emergency room. When the doctor asked Dad how he hurt his ankle, Dad said he wasn't looking where he was going and he stepped on one of Manny's trucks in the driveway.

I can kind of understand why Dad didn't want to tell the truth. One time I broke my wrist, and I told everyone I broke it in a fistfight. What REALLY happened was that I tried to stand up after my legs fell asleep from sitting on the toilet too long. But I liked my version better.

So it's only been a few days without Mum, and things are already starting to fall apart. We've got one serious injury so far, and who knows what's in store down the road.

Thursday
We brought back leftovers from the Spaghetti Barn, and that's what we had for dinner tonight. Dad had to stay late at work, so he called Rodrick and told him to warm up everyone's spaghetti in the microwave.

Rodrick gave me my plate first, and when he did, he said —

I blew on my spaghetti for a while to cool it down. But what I didn't know was that Rodrick never actually heated my spaghetti in the microwave — he just pretended to.

So when I bit into a meatball, it was ICE cold.

After that experience, I doubt I'll ever be able to eat leftovers again.

And the packed lunch thing isn't working out, either. This week Rodrick was in charge of making lunches, and he wrote a note on my bag, just like Mum does.

I didn't even bother eating the sandwich, since I've never seen Rodrick wash his hands even once.

My chore for the week is laundry, and I can't wait until my shift is over. For the record, I think it should be illegal for a boy to have to fold his mother's underwear.

Friday

One of the big changes with Mum going to school is that now Dad's in charge of helping me with my homework. No offense to Dad, but Mum is WAY better at homework help than he is. When Mum helps me do my homework, she basically gives me all the answers, and I'm in and out in ten minutes.

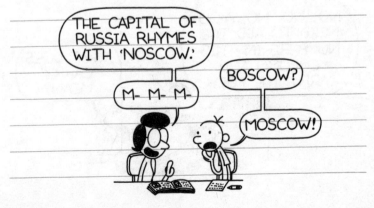

It's a whole different story with Dad. He wants to teach me HOW to do the work, and that's a lot more time-consuming. Plus, it's been a long time since Dad was in school, so I have to sit there and wait while he reads my textbooks and gets caught up.

But maths is the WORST. I guess the way they teach maths these days is totally different from the way they taught it when Dad was a kid, so he gets frustrated with the new rules and starts trying to teach me the way HE learned it.

Dad also licks his finger and his thumb to make it easier for him to turn the pages. And when he does that, I try and keep track of which pages he turns so I don't touch his spit.

But with all those numbers in my head, it doesn't leave a lot of room for maths facts.

I can tell when I've done something wrong, because Dad gets kind of frustrated with me and breathes real heavy out of his nose. So I've learned to put a tea towel on my arm whenever we're working on Algebra.

By the time it's over, two hours have gone by and it's time for me to go to bed. All I can say is, I hope Mum wraps up her classes pretty quick, because I'm a person who really needs his TV time at night.

Monday

This maths thing is becoming a problem. We have 'standardised testing' coming up at my school, and I heard that the teachers won't get their bonuses unless we get good scores. So there's a lot of pressure on us kids, which kind of stinks. I remember back in kindergarten, maths used to be really FUN.

Mrs Mackelroy says that if we don't do well on the test, we'll lose our budget and music class will turn into detention, or something like that. But I don't think kids are really getting the message. A few weeks ago we had a maths quiz, and Mrs Mackelroy said it was 'open notebook', which meant we could use our notes and textbooks to help us out.

Then she left the classroom to take care of something, and the second she stepped out the door, it was total chaos.

Practically everybody failed the quiz because people were using their notebook paper and books as ammunition.

So, based on that episode, I don't think Mrs Mackelroy had better make any big plans for how she's gonna spend her bonus.

OCTOBER

Tuesday

Tonight Dad walked up to me while I was sitting on the couch, and he seemed bent out of shape about something. He wanted to know why I didn't bring out the recycling bin this morning like he asked me to.

I told him he must be confused, because he never said anything to me about the recycling. But he said he asked me to do it last night while I was playing video games, and to be honest with you, that did seem a little familiar.

If I DID forget, it wasn't my fault. I actually have a really GREAT system for remembering things.

You know how some people leave notes for themselves when they need to remember something? Well, I think that's a lot of work, and it's a waste of paper, too.

So let's say I'm in bed and Mum walks into my room and tells me I have to bring a permission slip to school in the morning. I don't get out of bed and write a note.

I just throw one of my pillows across the room.

Then, when I wake up in the morning and go to walk out the door, I see the pillow and think, 'Hey, what's this pillow doing here?'

Then I remember, 'Oh yeah, I have to bring a permission slip to school'. See what I mean? It's totally foolproof.

Now that I think of it, I DID leave myself a reminder to take out the recycling. I SPECIFICALLY remember putting my socks on the TV before I went to bed, to remind myself in the morning.

And if Dad did something to mess up my system, he's only got himself to blame.

But Dad wouldn't let it go. He said now that I'm getting older, I need to start being more 'responsible'.

I've heard this sort of thing from Dad before. The last few weeks of the summer, our neighbour, Ms Grove, hired me to take care of her plants while she was on a business trip. Well, I did it for the first few days, and then I guess you could say I got busy with other things.

When Dad asked me how the plants were doing, I realised I hadn't been over there in at least a WEEK. I went to grab Ms Grove's key so I could water her plants, but the key wasn't in its usual spot.

I practically turned our house upside down looking for that key, but I couldn't find it.

It turns out the reason I couldn't find the key was because it wasn't in our house. I'd left it at Ms Grove's, and she found it when she got back from her trip.

Ms Grove was pretty mad that her key was in the front door, but the way I see it, she should've been happy nobody robbed her house.

She was mad about her plants, too, because unfortunately most of them didn't make it. I suggested that maybe she should buy a cactus or another plant that doesn't need a lot of water to survive.

That way, everything would be fine if I lost her key the NEXT time she went on a business trip.

But Ms Grove said she wouldn't hire me again even if her life depended on it. Then she sent me home without paying, which stinks, because I really did spend a lot of time looking for that key.

Anyway, I think that episode is still fresh in Dad's mind, and that's why I'm hearing this 'responsibility' thing again.

Hopefully, Dad will leave my socks on the television next time around and things won't get to this point.

Thursday

Well, Dad is really serious about me taking on more responsibility. And the first thing he wants me to do is start waking myself up in the morning.

That's actually a real problem, because I depend on HIM to wake me up.

That's the way we've been doing it for YEARS, and I really don't see any reason to change things now.

Dad said that if I don't learn to wake myself up with an alarm clock, then I'm not gonna know how to do it when I go off to college.

But I always figured that would be the way me and Dad would stay in touch.

Yesterday was the first day I tried to wake myself up, and it didn't work out so well. My alarm went off and all, but the sound just worked its way into my dream.

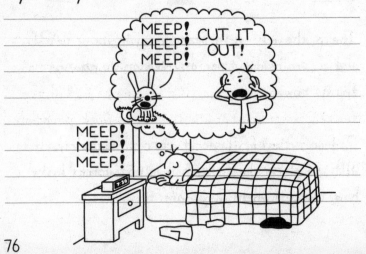

And today didn't go any better. I set my alarm to 'radio' and tuned it to a classical music station because I didn't want to hear that annoying beep first thing in the morning. But the music didn't wake me up, either.

The problem is, without an actual human being waking me up, my brain is always gonna find some excuse to keep sleeping. But I think I might've figured out a solution to this alarm clock situation. I found one of those old-style windup clocks in the storage room today, and those clocks make a huge racket when they go off.

I tested it out to see if it still worked, and sure enough, it did.

I don't think ANYONE could sleep through a noise like THAT. The only problem is that the clock doesn't have a 'snooze' bar, so I'm worried I'll shut it off and fall back asleep.

So tonight I hid the clock under my bed. This way, when the alarm goes off, I'll have to get up to find the clock, and then I'll be up for the day.

Friday
It turns out the new alarm clock caused some new problems.

With that windup clock ticking under my bed, I felt like I was sleeping on top of a bomb that was about to go off. So the stress kept me awake half the night.

I sleepwalked through my day at school, which was fine until we had an assembly. We were lined up to go into the auditorium, and I was leaning against the wall.

But I must've fallen asleep for half a second, because my hand slipped and I accidentally set off the fire alarm.

The whole school had to evacuate, and three minutes later there were a bunch of fire trucks out front.

After they found out there was no fire, they let everyone back into the school. The principal got on the loudspeaker and said that whoever set off the alarm was gonna be suspended and that they should turn themselves in.

I don't know much, but what I DO know is that you shouldn't announce what the punishment is gonna be BEFORE you ask people to turn themselves in. So I decided it would be smart to keep quiet and let this all blow over.

After third period, a rumour started going around school that the fire alarm squirts out invisible liquid when you pull the handle, and that the teachers had some sort of special X-ray wand they could use to see the liquid on somebody's hand. So it was only a matter of time before they found the culprit.

Then everyone started wondering if it was the TEACHERS who started the rumour and it was just a trick to see which kid would go to the bathroom first to wash his hands.

So that got everyone REALLY paranoid.

Then NOBODY would go to the bathroom, and everyone who actually needed to go decided to just hold it until the end of the day.

The principal eventually had to shut the school down early because nobody was washing their hands and we're right in the middle of flu season.

Mum was off at the library studying, so I had to call Dad at work and ask him to come pick me up from school early. And he didn't seem too happy about it.

But if he didn't make me wake myself up, none of this would've even happened.

Wednesday
They're starting a new unit in our Health class called 'The Facts of Life', and apparently it covers all the stuff they've been dancing around for the past couple of months. They sent permission slips home, and if you don't get yours signed, you're not allowed to even be in the classroom for the rest of the semester.

I really don't like this permission slip thing. Mum only lets me watch G-rated movies, so I know there's no WAY she'll let me be in the class.

To get around that problem, I typed up a fake note and taped it on top of the actual permission slip.

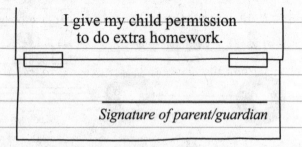

I give my child permission
to do extra homework.

Signature of parent/guardian

Luckily, Mum didn't look at the paper too closely, and I got the signature I needed.

I'm actually glad they're doing this 'Facts of Life' unit, because I have a lot of questions about this stuff, and I don't have a reliable way of getting answers.

Just about everything I know in this department comes from Albert Sandy, and I'm starting to wonder if he's been feeding me bad information. Like last week, he told everyone at the lunch table that it's medically impossible for a girl to fart.

Well, I know that's not true because of the time Mum hugged Aunt Dorothy on Christmas Eve.

TOOT!

Anyway, today was the first day of the 'Facts of Life' unit, and sure enough, Nurse Powell sent the kids whose parents wouldn't sign their permission slips down to the library to be 'special helpers' for the day.

The rest of us were pretty excited, because we couldn't wait to hear all the juicy stuff Nurse Powell was about to tell us.

But it didn't go the way I expected at ALL. Nurse Powell put some charts up on the easel and started talking about 'zygotes' and 'chromosomes' and a whole bunch of other scientific nonsense.

I kept waiting for her to tell us this was all a big joke and then get to the good stuff, but it never happened. So I'm guessing the school is just trying to confuse us to make us lose interest.

Anyway, if the school IS trying to confuse us, they're doing a pretty good job. At lunch we tried to explain what we learned in the 'Facts of Life' unit to the kids who didn't get their permission slips signed, and we couldn't agree on a single thing.

<u>Saturday</u>
Another thing Dad's in charge of now that Mum's
back in school is taking us kids to our dentist
appointments.

Most kids don't like going to the dentist, but I
actually look FORWARD to it. I've been going
to the same dentist since I was two years old,
and they are totally my type of operation.

But the main reason I like going to the dentist
is because I am TOTALLY in love with the nurse
who works there, Rachel.

Rachel always lectures me about brushing and flossing and all that, but she's so cute that it's hard to take her seriously.

Mum's always getting after me about flossing, too. She says that if I don't take better care of my teeth, I'm gonna end up with dentures before I go to college.

I've been thinking about that, and maybe false teeth wouldn't be such a bad thing.

If I had dentures, I could have someone ELSE take care of my teeth, and I could spend the extra time doing something I actually enjoy.

The only problem with being in love with your dental nurse is that you only get to see her every six months when you get your teeth cleaned. So I have to make the most of every visit.

The last time I had an appointment, I looked Rachel in the eye the whole time she cleaned my teeth so she could see I was definitely interested.

This morning I actually went out and bought
some cologne to make an extra-good impression
on her. So when Dad told me to get in the car,
I was ready.

But Dad drove right past my dentist's office and
got on the highway. I told him that he had
missed the turn and that Tender Hugs Dental
Care was back the other way.

But Dad said I'm 'too old' to keep going to a kids' dentist, so starting today he was switching me over to his dentist, Dr Kagan.

I got a chill up my spine when he said that name. I've seen Dr Kagan's billboards on the highway, and I get the impression he has a totally different approach than Tender Hugs.

DR SALAZAR KAGAN
ORAL SURGERY
and general dentistry

ROOT CANALS
ABSCESS DRAINAGE
BONE GRAFTING

'Because bad oral health is nothing to smile about.'

I tried to get Dad to change his mind, but he said he already did the paperwork to switch me over and there was no turning back. I thought about making a run for it, but Dad must've known what I was thinking, because he locked the car doors.

Dr Kagan's office was even scarier than I pictured it. He didn't have any colouring books or toys or the kinds of things they have in the Tender Hugs waiting room.

Dr Kagan was waiting for me in his office, and all his sharp metal instruments and drills were right out in the open for me to see when I walked in.

So I could tell this guy wasn't fooling around.

After I sat down in the chair, Dr Kagan started grilling me about my eating and drinking habits. He actually got MAD when I told him I drink soda, and he went in the side room and brought out a jar filled with brown liquid that had a rotten tooth in it.

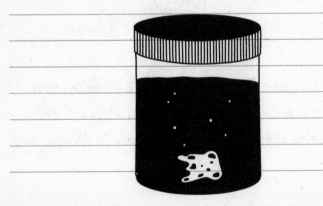

He told me this is what happened to a real tooth when it was left in a jar of soda for twenty-four hours. I told Dr Kagan I would make sure I never left my teeth in a jar of soda overnight. I'm pretty sure he thought I was being sarcastic, but I was just trying to show him I was paying attention.

Then he cleaned my teeth. I started to panic, because if there's one person you don't want to be mad at you, it's the guy who's got metal tools poking around in your mouth.

At one point, Dr Kagan started doing X-rays. He put a piece of plastic between my teeth and told me to bite down. Then he took an X-ray and got the next piece of plastic ready.

After two or three X-rays, I started to get the hang of it, and so when Dr Kagan did my molars, I bit down on the plastic before he even told me to. At least I THOUGHT it was the plastic. It turns out it was actually Dr Kagan's finger.

Well, if he was mad before, it was NOTHING compared to this.

Dr Kagan told me to go out to the waiting room while he worked on my 'diagnosis'. I was pretty sure he was gonna come back and tell Dad I needed to get a root canal or something so he could get even with me.

But Dr Kagan actually did something even WORSE. He told Dad I needed to take 'major corrective measures' for my overbite, and he gave Dad this pamphlet –

Your Child Needs

HEADGEAR

Dr Kagan said I would need to wear my headgear at all times, especially during the day when I'm at school. So obviously he's trying to ruin my social life.

Monday

When I woke up this morning, I couldn't find my headgear where I left it, so I had to go to school without it. Not that I'm complaining or anything.

In Health class Nurse Powell told us we were going to be starting a new unit about parenting. She said that being a mother or a father is a big responsibility and that in this unit we were gonna learn that taking care of a baby is no piece of cake.

Then she took out a carton of eggs. She said each one of us was gonna have to take our egg home and return it to class the next day.

And the rule was that we had to return our egg to her in perfect shape, with no cracks in it or anything.

Now, I don't know what a chicken egg has to do with a baby, but this is one of those situations that make me wonder if I'd be getting a better education if Mum and Dad switched me over to private school.

Then Nurse Powell said this egg thing was gonna count for 25% of our grade.

Well, when Nurse Powell mentioned grades, I got really nervous. I'm already failing Algebra, and I don't need to flunk out of Health, too. So I knew I was gonna have to keep my egg safe.

The other boys didn't seem too worried about THEIR grades, judging by what happened after class let out.

I heard it took the janitor all afternoon to scrub the yolks off the lockers.

The only boy besides me who didn't break his egg right away was Rowley, who tucked it in his shirt pocket.

I didn't have a shirt pocket or anywhere safe to put MY egg, so I needed to figure out something quick.

I ended up getting a huge wad of toilet paper from the bathroom and stuffing it into my backpack for cushioning. I had to take some of my books out so they wouldn't crush the egg, so I guess that means I won't be doing my History homework tonight.

STUFF
STUFF

I'm nervous around eggs anyway, because of an incident that happened last year.

My family got invited to the Snellas' house for another one of their kids' half-birthday parties. The Snellas had a table set up with all sorts of food, and most of it looked too fancy for me. But I knew Mum would think it was rude if I didn't put something on my plate.

The only thing I could actually recognise was the devilled eggs, because I had them at Gramma's house a couple of times.

I put about ten of them on my plate. But when I bit into one, I gagged. The devilled eggs at the Snellas' house didn't taste ANYTHING like the ones Gramma makes, and now I had a whole plate full of them.

So I waited until no one was looking, and then I dumped all the devilled eggs in this plastic plant in the dining room.

DUMP

I got away with it, but a few weeks later Mrs Snella told Mum there was a really bad smell in their house and they couldn't figure out where it was coming from.

At first Mr and Mrs Snella thought the smell was coming from the carpet, so they hired a cleaner to come shampoo the rug. But that didn't solve the problem, and they thought maybe a squirrel or a mouse died in their walls. So they had a carpenter come in to try to find it.

After a few weeks, I guess they couldn't take the smell anymore, so they moved out.

And I have to admit I felt a little bit guilty when I saw they were taking their plastic plant with them.

Ever since, I've been trying to figure out how to sneak some devilled eggs into Fregley's house.

Tuesday
Yesterday when I got home, I put my egg in my sock drawer, but then I realised it wouldn't be safe in there.

Whenever I have something new, Manny finds a way to get to it and wreck it.

In fact, it only took a day and a half for Manny to find my headgear. And I don't care WHAT Dr Kagan says, there's no way I'm putting THAT thing in my mouth again.

I thought about hiding the egg at the top of my closet, but that wouldn't stop Manny. I hid some comic books up there once, but that boy can climb like a monkey.

What I realised is that the more work I
put into hiding something, the better chance
Manny has of finding it. So I decided to hide
my egg in an obvious spot where he would never
think to look.

I put it in the refrigerator on the second shelf.
But this morning I opened the refrigerator to
get my egg, and it wasn't where I left it.

I went into a panic, and I asked Mum if she'd
seen Manny take my egg out of the refrigerator.

But Mum said SHE was the one who took it, and
that's what she was making me for breakfast.

All of a sudden I felt a little sick to my stomach. I realised that if I couldn't even take care of an egg for twenty-four hours, I definitely have no business ever being a parent.

When I got to school, I noticed that all the girls in my Health class had gotten THEIR eggs to school safely. Some of the girls were carrying theirs around in little pouches they'd sewn, and a few of them had even accessorised their eggs with sparkles and glitter and stuff like that.

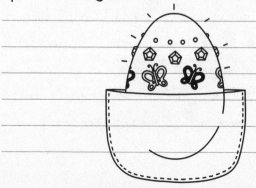

I'm pretty sure the point of the lesson was to teach us how hard it is to take care of a baby, so I don't think the girls were really getting the message.

I was thinking about swiping Rowley's egg when he wasn't looking and passing it off as my own, but he had drawn all over his in crayon, so that wasn't an option.

ROWLEY JR.

When Nurse Powell came to my desk, I pulled out the plastic baggie that had my scrambled egg in it, but she didn't seem too impressed.

So I guess that means I'm probably gonna be in summer school to repeat Health class.

Nurse Powell congratulated everyone who kept their eggs in perfect condition overnight. Then she collected all the eggs and threw them in the trash.

Well, that sent Rowley and the girls into hysterics.

All I can say is, this whole episode has got me seriously concerned about the next generation of parents in our country.

Friday
This afternoon there was a knock on the door, and when I opened it I was pretty surprised to see Grandpa standing there.

I was kind of confused, because he had his overnight bag with him. But when I turned around and saw Mum and Dad with THEIR luggage, I figured out what was going on.

Mum and Dad said they haven't gotten to spend a lot of time together lately, so they decided to go on a 'romantic weekend getaway'. They asked Grandpa to come by and watch us while they were gone.

I wish they didn't have to go and throw the word 'romantic' in there, because that part was definitely too much information for me.

Mum and Dad don't trust me and Rodrick to be home alone, because the LAST time they left us on our own, Rodrick had a huge party.

Whenever Mum and Dad go away, they usually leave us with Gramma. But Gramma's on a cruise with her friends, so that's why we got stuck with Grandpa.

Mum and Dad don't give us any advance warning when they go away. For their anniversary, we didn't even know they were gone until they called.

The LAST time they left us at our own house with Grandpa was when me and Rodrick were really little. I don't remember everything that went wrong that week, but I do remember that he dropped me off for T-ball practice at the wrong time and at the wrong field.

I don't think Rodrick was crazy about the idea of having Grandpa as a babysitter, because the second Mum and Dad left, Rodrick took off.

SCREECH

LOADED DIPER

Unfortunately, I don't have a van or a driver's licence of my own, so I was stuck with Grandpa and Manny.

LET'S PLAY GIN RUMMY!

SHUFFLE

Manny went straight to bed, even though it was only 4:30 in the afternoon. So that left just me and Grandpa.

Grandpa made toasted cheese sandwiches with the crusts cut off for dinner, which I haven't had since I was really little. We watched some TV, but then at 7:00 Grandpa shut it off and asked me if I wanted him to read me a story. I haven't had a bedtime story since I was in kindergarten, but I didn't wanna hurt Grandpa's feelings, so I just went along with it.

Saturday
Since I went to bed at 7:30 last night, I woke up really early this morning.

And when I came downstairs, I saw a big white binder sitting out on the kitchen table.

TAKING CARE OF
Gregory & Rodrick

A to Z

All of a sudden the toasted cheese sandwiches and the story and the early bedtime all made sense. Grandpa was using the manual Mum made for him the LAST time he took care of us at home, eight or nine years ago.

I flipped through the pages, and sure enough, it was filled with instructions for how to take care of us when we were little kids.

And at least 95% of it was totally outdated.

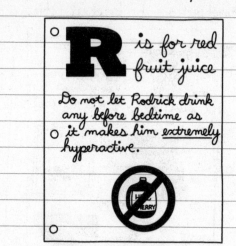

Some of the stuff in there was actually pretty embarrassing. I'm just glad I found the manual before Rodrick did, or he'd never let me hear the end of it.

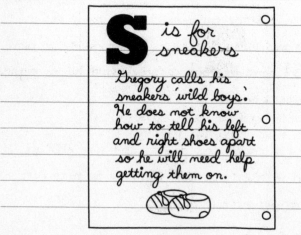

I flipped to the page with 'T' on it, and here's what I found —

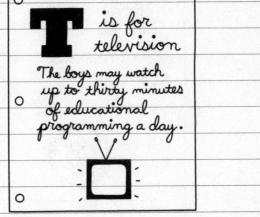

T is for
television

The boys may watch up to thirty minutes of educational programming a day.

I don't think I'm gonna survive a whole weekend with Grandpa if I'm not allowed to watch a lot of TV, so I ripped out the page and drew up a new one.

T is for
television

Gregory is allowed to watch as much as he likes.

Then I realised that the 'S' page was on the back of the 'T' page, so I had to replace that one, too.

S is for
spanking

It's what you should do to Rodrick if he ever leaves the house with-out asking first.

Monday
Unfortunately, Mum and Dad got home before Rodrick did yesterday, and Grandpa went back to his condo. Which is a shame, because I was really keeping my fingers crossed on that 'S' thing.

Mum said that she and Dad did a lot of talking over the weekend, and they agreed that things have started to slip around the house ever since she started going back to school.

I figured Mum was gonna chew us guys out for not doing our share, but she actually said she was gonna HIRE someone to help with the cleaning. I couldn't believe what I was hearing. The words Mum used were 'domestic help', but I knew that was just code for 'maid'.

I guess Mum was pretty embarrassed about having to hire someone to help out with the household chores, because she asked us all not to mention it to anyone.

Well, I'm sorry, but opportunities like this don't come around too often for me, so it was a little hard to keep quiet at school.

WE'RE GETTING A MAID!

Chirag Gupta said his family doesn't NEED a maid and that he was glad his mum is there when he comes home from school every day.

But I'm sure that's what all the non-maid people say to make themselves feel better.

Tomorrow is our maid Isabella's first day. I thought that meant we could all kick back and be a little extra slobby, since someone would be picking up after us, but Mum made everyone clean the house tonight. She said she didn't want Isabella thinking we lived in a 'pigsty'.

Tuesday

Today when I got home from school, Isabella was in the family room watching a talk show. I guess I can't really blame her for loafing around, since we had done all the cleaning for her. But she stayed for about two hours and totally hogged the TV.

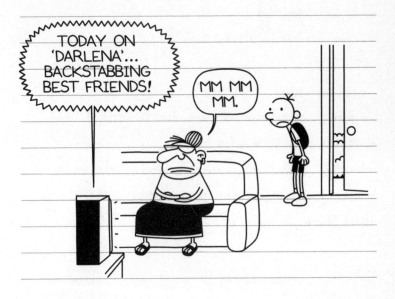

Tonight when Mum got home after her classes, she was amazed at how spotless the house was. I don't think she remembered that WE were the ones who did all the work.

But she seemed happy, so I didn't want to spoil it for her.

I wasn't as happy as Mum. Last night I left Isabella a note asking her to take care of my laundry. I wasn't sure if she would take orders from a kid, so I made the note look like it was from Mum.

Dear Isabella,
    Please do my son
    Gregory's laundry.

      Sincerely,
      Mrs Heffley

I'm technically supposed to do my OWN laundry, and I didn't want Mum to find out I was asking Isabella to do it for me. So I put this line at the bottom —

P.S. Now that you've read my note, you should just throw it out.

Then I put the note on top of the bag and left it out where Isabella would see it. I was expecting to come home and find all my laundry in neat, folded piles on my bed, but instead I got a note BACK from Isabella.

Luckily, I got home before Mum did, or she would've found it.

Dear Mrs Heffley,
Now, which child is Gregory again?
—Isabella

That really stunk, because I had to haul my laundry bag all the way back upstairs. And let me tell you, it was a lot harder going up than coming down.

Isabella doesn't come back until Thursday, so I guess I'll have to wait until then to take another crack at it.

This is actually pretty exciting for me, because I've never had anyone I could farm my work out to. Rodrick is ALWAYS tricking me into doing stuff for HIM.

He'll start by asking me to do something, and I always say no.

Then he starts counting down from ten. And I don't know why, but that gets to me every time.

I've found out that kind of thing doesn't work on adults.

Last week I tried to get Dad to fetch the TV remote, because I left it on the kitchen table. But he didn't even move a muscle.

Anyway, I'm hoping Isabella comes through for me on Thursday. I've been wearing the same socks for a few days now, and they're starting to feel like cardboard.

Thursday
OK, now this is starting to get a little ridiculous. Last night I dragged my laundry back downstairs and left another note for Isabella.

> Dear Isabella,
> Gregory is the child whose bedroom
> has blue wallpaper. Please wash
> and dry his clothes and put them
> in his room.
>
> Thank you,
> Mrs Heffley

But instead of clean laundry, I just got
another note.

> Dear Mrs Heffley,
> Thank you for the clarification. Now,
> would you like me to separate the
> darks from the lights or wash them
> all together?
>
> Isabella

Now I get Isabella's act. She's gonna keep
dragging this out forever. On the one hand, I
kind of have to respect her skill at avoiding work.
But on the other hand, I really do need some
clean underwear soon.

And what REALLY stinks is that Isabella has been eating our junk food. I went to get some pretzels out of the pantry tonight, and the bag was practically empty.

I noticed the potato chips were gone, too. And believe it or not, Isabella left a note in the pantry to complain about our snack selection.

Dear Mrs Heffley,
    Please note that I prefer barbecue potato chips over plain ones.
                    —Isabella

Well, the potato chips she ate WERE barbecue, but she just didn't know it. Manny licks the flavoring off the barbecue chips and puts them back in the bag. Unfortunately, I had to learn that the hard way.

Mum went out and bought a bunch of snacks just for Isabella and put them in the pantry, and the rest of us aren't allowed to touch them.

Monday

Today at school they announced that they're going to have a special fundraiser for the music program, called a 'Lock-In'. From what I can tell, it's sort of like a big boy-girl slumber party, so you can definitely count ME in.

The only thing that bothered me was the 'chaperone' part. So I cut that out before I showed it to Mum.

Tuesday

All right, I've had it with our maid. I gave her one more shot at doing my laundry, and she weaselled out of it again.

> Dear Isabella,
> It is fine to mix the lights and darks together. Please take care of this at your earliest convenience as Gregory is out of clean clothes for school.
>
> Mrs Heffley

This is what I found sitting on top of the laundry bag when I got home –

Dear Mrs Heffley,
Thank you for the clarification on how to handle the lights and the darks. Unfortunately, I have misplaced your earlier note in which you stated who Gregory is.

—Isabella

I officially give up. Since we always clean the house before Isabella comes, I'm pretty sure the only 'work' she does is writing these notes.

And it gets worse. When I got into bed tonight, I felt something at the bottom of my sheets. So I reached down and found what I think was a pantyhose sock.

That means Isabella has been taking naps in MY BED. I went into Mum's room and told her that I think she made a mistake hiring Isabella and that she should let her go.

But Mum didn't want to hear it. She said that the house has been 'immaculate' ever since we hired her and that everyone should be grateful for the work she's doing for us. So Isabella's got Mum TOTALLY fooled.

All I can say is, if being a maid means watching TV all day, eating snacks, and taking naps in my bed, then I guess I've finally found a career I can get excited about.

NOVEMBER

Saturday

Dad dropped me off at school at 8:00 last night for the Lock-In, and the second I walked through the door, I knew I made a huge mistake. It was, like, 90% boys and 10% girls. And even worse, ROWLEY was there.

I turned to leave, but one of the chaperones had already locked the door. So I was stuck there for the night with everyone else.

I'm guessing most of the girls in my class decided not to go to the Lock-In and the ones who DID show up just didn't get the word in time.

I decided I was gonna have to make the most of it, and I walked into the auditorium, where everyone else was taking their stuff. The first thing I noticed was that there was at least one adult for every kid, which is not really a great recipe for wild times.

Most of the chaperones were parents, but a few of them were teachers. And something tells me the teachers were only there because they didn't have a choice.

I plopped my stuff down on the stage, where all the other kids were. Then I noticed that Rowley was there, so I moved my stuff to the other side of the stage.

I think most of the kids had already written off the night, because just about everyone was playing with whatever electronic gadget they brought with them.

I didn't even THINK of bringing my video games, and I didn't have a magazine or anything to entertain myself. So I asked one of the grown-ups what I could do.

Mrs Barnum told me there was an 'activity centre' in the corner for anyone who needed to take a 'fun break' during the night.

But all of the activities were little-kid stuff.

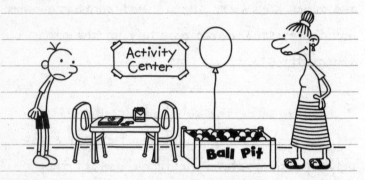

I decided to just sit on my sleeping bag with my hands folded on my lap instead.

At 9:00 the adults said it was time for 'party games', but nobody heard them because everyone had headphones on. Mr Tanner said people needed to be 'social', so he confiscated all the mobile phones, music players, and whatever else kids had and put them in a garbage bag.

Then we all sat in a circle in the middle of the auditorium. Mrs Carr said we were gonna play some 'icebreakers' that would help us get to know each other better.

But the truth is, all of us kids know one another really well, because we've been together since preschool. In fact, I think we know each other TOO well.

Mrs Carr said we were gonna start with something called the 'Name Game', where everyone goes around and gives themselves a nickname that starts with the same letter as their first name, like 'Sporty Seth' or 'Funny Fred' or something like that. The idea was that your nickname would say something about your personality.

Rowley went first.

It was really stressful trying to come up with a cool-sounding nickname, and my turn was coming up quick. I finally settled on 'Great Greg', which I know is a little lame, but it was hard to think of a decent nickname that starts with the letter 'G'.

I guess the kid to my right, George Fleer, was having the same problem as me.

I couldn't use the same word as George or people would think I was copying him.

So I sat there for a while trying to think of
another good 'G' word, but everyone was staring
at me and my mind just went blank.

Then Mrs Libby chimed in to try and bail me out.

Everyone seemed pretty happy with that, even
though 'Jolly' doesn't start with the letter 'G.'
And it makes you wonder about our education
system, especially since Mrs Libby is the eighth-
grade honours English teacher.

I thought 'Jolly Greg' was a TERRIBLE
nickname, but before I could come up with
something better, the person to my left went,
and it was too late.

So now I was stuck with a stupid nickname for the rest of the night, and probably until I go off to college.

After that, we played a game called 'I Never Told Anyone This Before', where we had to tell everyone a secret. Mrs Carr said the game would help us 'bond' with one another, but I think the REAL purpose was to let the chaperones know who the troublemakers were.

My theory was proven right later on when Teddy Caldwell went down the hall to the bathroom and a chaperone trailed him.

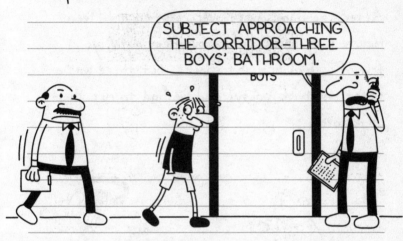

We played a few more icebreakers, but nobody could concentrate, because every five seconds one of the mobile phones in the electronics bag would start buzzing or ringing. Then Mr Tanner would fish through the bag and try to find the phone that was ringing so he could shut it off.

Eventually he just gave up and locked the bag in the teachers' lounge.

After the games were over, we had a fifteen-minute rest-break before our next activity. A few of us had brought snacks, but there was a strict no-snack policy, and we had to eat them undercover.

The chaperones seemed to know EXACTLY who had the snacks, and they confiscated about 95% of them. Mr Farley even found my cherry sour balls, which were hidden in my pillowcase.

We finally realised that a mole was ratting us out. It was Justin Spitzer, and he was being paid off with the snacks the adults collected.

The only kid who still had junk food was Jeffrey Chang, who had a huge bag of cheese puffs. I think Jeffrey knew it was just a matter of time before he was caught, so he locked himself in the boys' bathroom and tried to enjoy his snack. But the adults figured out what was going on, and Jeffrey panicked and got rid of the evidence.

After our break we got back into the circle, and Mrs Dean told us we were gonna play a new game called 'Guess Who?' Then she split us up into ten teams. I was on Team Three with George Fleer, Tyson Sanders, and a few other kids.

I was just glad I didn't have to be on the same team as Rowley, because that would've been totally uncomfortable.

Here's how the game worked: Each team had to go into another room and take a picture of one of its members. But the picture had to be a close-up, like of an ear or a nose or a hand or something like that. Then each team would bring their picture to the library, and the other teams would have to guess who was in the picture.

Then Mrs Dean said the winning team would get ice cream sandwiches from the freezer in the cafeteria. I have to admit, it sounded like a fun game. But when she handed out the cameras, there was practically a riot, since it had been almost two hours since any of us had access to any kind of technology.

Then we found out they were those old-fashioned instant cameras that develop your pictures right away, and everyone was a little disappointed, because those kinds don't have a screen or anything.

Our team went down to the science lab, where we could take our photo in private. The first thing we had to do was figure out who was gonna be in the picture.

George Fleer said we should take a picture of his belly button. But everybody thought that would be too obvious because George has a serious outie, and all the other groups would know EXACTLY who it was.

We tried taking pictures of different kids in our group, but most of them were too obvious.

Nicky Wood wanted the picture to be of him, but he's totally covered in freckles and we couldn't find a single part of him that wouldn't be a dead giveaway.

We took a picture of Christopher Brownfield's
back, but we caught one of the Team Four kids
spying on us and we had to pick someone else.

HEY!

We took a bunch of pictures of Tyson Sanders,
but the best one was of his bent arm.

FLASH

You couldn't even tell what the picture was of, so that's the one we went with.

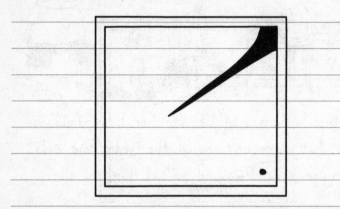

When all the teams got back together in the library, we put our picture up on the wall with everybody else's. And as soon as we saw the other pictures, we knew we were gonna win.

Some of the pictures were so easy to identify that it was actually kind of pathetic.

In fact, don't even ask me what the people on Rowley's team were thinking.

We were eager to get on with the guessing part of the game, since we knew nobody would be able to figure out who was in our picture. But Mr Tanner just stood there looking at our photograph.

Then Mr Tanner said that he didn't appreciate Team Three's 'juvenile stunt' and that we were disqualified from the competition.

We all looked at one another, trying to figure out what the heck Mr Tanner was talking about. But Mrs Dean was mad, too. She said it was completely inappropriate to take a picture of someone's 'posterior'.

No one on my team knew what 'posterior' meant, but luckily we were in the library, so we looked it up in the dictionary. And you'll never believe this, but it means 'bum'. In fact, we found out that there are about a million OTHER words for 'bum', too.

HEE HEE HEE HEE!

But the teachers were MAD. They actually thought we took a picture of somebody's bum, and I guess if you held the picture at a certain angle, you could see how a person could make a mistake like that.

Mr Tanner said he was gonna call our parents and tell them to come take us home, and he said that the kid whose bum was in the picture was gonna be in REALLY big trouble.

I knew that if Mr Tanner called my parents at 11:00 at night, they were not gonna be happy, and I could tell a lot of the other kids on my team were thinking the same thing. Then George Fleer made a run for it, which kind of put everyone into a panic.

So the rest of us ran, too.

It was every man for himself, and I ended up hiding in the music room with Tyson Sanders. We shut the lights off so nobody would come looking for us there.

Tyson was really worried that the teachers were gonna do a bum line-up to try and match the picture to the right kid. But I told Tyson he didn't have anything to worry about, because he pulls his pants all the way down when he uses the urinal, so everyone already knows what his bum looks like.

Me and Tyson were in the music room for a long time, but we were finally caught by a couple of teachers who used Justin Spitzer to sniff us out.

The chaperones brought us down to the library, where all the other Team Three members were already rounded up.

Well, everyone except Christopher Brownfield, who for all I know is still hiding behind the soda machine on the second floor.

Tyson told Mr Tanner that the picture was of his arm. Luckily, there's a mole near Tyson's elbow that matched up with the one in the picture, or I don't think Mr Tanner would've believed him.

After Mr Tanner looked at the picture and Tyson's arm a few more times, he said he had made an 'innocent mistake' and that any 'reasonable person' would have done the same thing. It seemed like a pretty lame apology to me, but I was just glad he wasn't still talking about calling our parents.

After that, the party games were over, and the adults said it was time for us to turn in for the night. I think everyone who went to the Lock-In was planning on staying up all night, but at this point I was glad to go to sleep if it meant the night might go by quicker.

I went to the auditorium to get into my sleeping bag, which was parked right next to Jennifer Houseman, who is actually not that bad-looking. But the grown-ups said the girls needed to take their stuff and move down the hall to the library media room and the boys had to stay in the auditorium.

I was hoping I could get some rest, but a lot of the guys started horsing around, and it was impossible to sleep.

At one point George Fleer started chasing people around with his outie, which was pretty terrifying.

See, this is the kind of thing I can't stand about boys my age. When it comes down to it, they're just a bunch of wild animals.

When George started chasing people around, I excused myself to go to the bathroom so I could brush my teeth. The bathroom is in the back of the auditorium, and the lights were off, so it was really dark back there.

I heard this weird noise, and I got a little freaked out for a second, because our school has a problem with rodents. But it turned out to just be Fregley playing by himself in the ball pit.

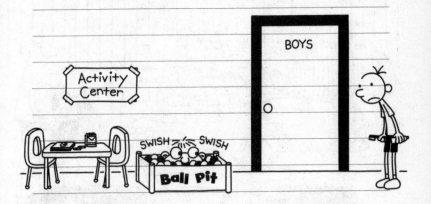

Around midnight Mr Palmero, the school guidance counsellor, told everyone to get into their sleeping bags and settle down. Then he said there was no talking for the rest of the night and he didn't want to hear a peep out of anyone.

Every once in a while, somebody would cut the cheese, and that made Mr Palmero really mad because he couldn't figure out who was doing it.

After what happened earlier with the pictures,
I think the grown-ups were just really sensitive
about anything having to do with bums.

Mr Palmero said that if anyone needed to 'pass
gas', they had to go behind the curtain on the
stage to do it.

So then a lot of the boys started taking turns
telling Mr Palmero they needed to go behind the
curtain, and then they'd make the most obnoxious
noises you can imagine.

That went on for a while, and it kind of reached its peak when David Rosenburg went down to the music room and brought back a tuba.

I don't know if it was a coincidence or not, but right about that time the heat went off in the auditorium.

In fact, I think someone turned the air-conditioner on. All I know is that everyone stayed in their sleeping bags after that.

After a while Mr Palmero fell asleep, but all the boys were still awake. Some guys were saying this was like prison, and people were talking about busting out of there and going home.

The problem was that all the exits were padlocked. I guess we should've known what we were getting into when they called this thing a 'Lock-In.'

Albert Sandy said he'd seen a movie where some guy busted out of prison with a spoon, and a lot of people got pretty excited about that idea.

But it turns out that was just a bunch of Hollywood baloney, because we got some spoons from the kitchen and we couldn't even make a DENT in the linoleum floor.

At about 1:30 in the morning, someone noticed flashing lights coming from outside, so we all went to the back of the auditorium to see what was going on.

There was a guy from the tow truck company, and he was walking around Mr Palmero's car, which was parked in a handicapped spot.

We tried to get the towing guy's attention so he could break us out of the school.

But the guy never heard us, and he towed Mr Palmero's car. I thought about waking Mr Palmero up to tell him, but I figured we should just let him get his rest.

By this time it was so cold in the auditorium that us boys packed ourselves together like sardines to preserve body heat.

I figured it was probably nice and toasty in the library media room, and I was seriously thinking about going back there and joining the girls.

But I figured I'd get caught and I'd just be back where I started.

I think I probably fell asleep around 2:30. Then at 3:00 there was a pounding on the back door that woke everybody up. Mr Palmero unlocked the door, and there was a bunch of angry parents standing outside.

Apparently, they'd been trying to call their kids to make sure everything was OK, but the kids weren't answering, because Mr Tanner took everyone's mobile phones. So then the parents called one another and everyone got all in a panic.

To make a long story short, the parents who came to the school took their kids home with them. And that left the only two kids who didn't have their own mobile phones: me and Rowley. So that was pretty awkward.

Something tells me this whole Lock-In idea was just a scheme set up by the parents and teachers to turn us kids off to boy-girl parties. And if that's true, then mission accomplished.

<u>Monday</u>

I spent the weekend trying to recover from the Lock-In, since I got zero sleep on Friday night. But I think the whole experience was just too much for my body, because this morning when I woke up, I was sick.

I admit I've faked being sick before to get out of going to school, but usually Mum calls my bluff.

But today Mum took my temperature, and I guess it must've been pretty high, because she said I needed to stay in bed.

She said she had to spend the day at the library to study for her final test tonight and she wouldn't be able to stay home to take care of me. Well, that kind of stunk, because the only good thing about being sick is having someone fuss over you.

Mum said Isabella was working today and that if there was an emergency, I could go to her. But after Mum left, I locked my bedroom door because I was afraid Isabella might try to come into my room to take her nap.

I must've dozed off around noon, and when I woke up, there was a lot of commotion downstairs. The TV was turned up really loud, and I could hear what sounded like a bunch of women talking.

I looked out the window, and there were a ton of cars in the driveway and on the street.

I didn't know what was going on, so I just stayed in my room. About a half hour later, Mum pulled up in her car and went inside the house. Five minutes after that, all these women streamed out the door, including Isabella.

Mum walked upstairs to my room, and she was really steamed.

She said she decided to come home early from the
library to take care of me, and when she did, she
walked in on a soap opera viewing party with all
the maids from the neighborhood.

Tonight Mum had another house-meeting and
said that Isabella's services would 'no longer be
required' and that we were all going to have to
pitch in around the house. I was happy to hear
that, because now I can stop checking my bed for
pantyhose socks.

<u>Tuesday</u>

When I got to school today, Rowley was waiting
by my locker, and he had a huge smile on his face.
Then I noticed he had a big pimple right in the
middle of his forehead.

Most people would have stayed home from school
if they had a zit like that, but here's what
Rowley said —

Well, that really irked me for some reason. But that wasn't the end of it.

Later on in the day I saw Rowley hanging out near the older kids' lockers. So I guess he thinks just because he got a pimple, he's part of their club now or something.

'SUP, FELLAS?

I think it's really pathetic that Rowley's trying to impress people with his stupid zit.

And believe me, I'm not jealous or anything. But this is a kid who still sleeps with a pile of stuffed animals every night, so it doesn't make any sense that he would get his first pimple before I got MINE.

I will say the whole episode has got me thinking. I've been waiting to hit my growth spurt or at least start growing some facial hair, but things have been kind of slow going.

And now that Rowley's got a pimple, I'm kind of anxious to get things moving along.

When I got home from school today, I checked myself in the mirror to see if anything seemed different. But everything looked exactly the same as it always does.

So after dinner I asked Mum and Dad when I could expect things to start happening.

But they told me that when they were my age, they were WAY behind their classmates when it came to this sort of thing.

Then Dad told me not to expect to get a lot of facial hair even when I'm an adult, because he's a grown man and he only needs to shave once or twice a week.

Well, that was some REALLY bad news. People are always saying you can grow up and be anything you want, but now I realise that's not true.

I can name at least half a dozen jobs I can never have if I can't grow a beard or a mustache or at least some decent stubble.

MAGICIAN   PIRATE   LUMBERJACK

ARTIST   COP   CRIMINAL

Wednesday

Today was day two of Rowley's pimple, and he was walking around with his hair parted like a curtain so everyone could get an eyeful of his zit.

I couldn't really take another day of this, and I decided to do something about it. So I wrote a note and handed it to him in the hallway.

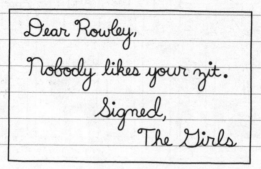

And I'm happy to say my note did the trick.

But right before lunchtime something totally crazy happened. Our class was heading to the cafeteria, and when we walked through the hallway where the older kids have their lockers, Jordan Jury was standing there with a few of his friends.

Jordan stopped us and said —

I couldn't believe it. Like I said before, Jordan Jury's parties are LEGENDARY.

But the best thing about Jordan Jury's parties is that there are GIRLS there, which means his parties are totally different from the kind I usually get invited to.

ZAP

The point is, this is a REAL party we're talking about, and not like the Lock-In, where there were a million chaperones running the show.

I have no idea why Jordan Jury invited me and Rowley to his party. It could've been my maths book or Rowley's zit or both.

But it was pretty clear that he thought me and Rowley were friends and that the invitation was a package deal.

And I didn't want to do anything that might change his mind.

I can definitely pretend I'm friends with Rowley for one night if it means I get to play 'Spin the Bottle' with a bunch of girls who are a whole grade ahead of me.

Thursday

You'll never believe this, but Mum's not letting me go to Jordan Jury's party.

And it's not because it's a boy-girl party or because a bunch of older kids are gonna be there. It's because Uncle Gary's WEDDING is this weekend.

This has got to be some kind of world record for bad timing. I begged Mum to let me stay home and go to the party, but she wouldn't budge, even after I promised I'd go to Uncle Gary's NEXT wedding.

Mum said I can't skip it, because I'm in the wedding party and I can't let Uncle Gary down.

The thing is, I've been in Uncle Gary's wedding party every single time, and I'll tell you exactly how THAT'S gonna go.

Uncle Gary's gonna ask me to be a 'reader'. Adults always pick a kid to read something from the Old Testament at weddings because everyone thinks it's cute when the kid can't pronounce the names.

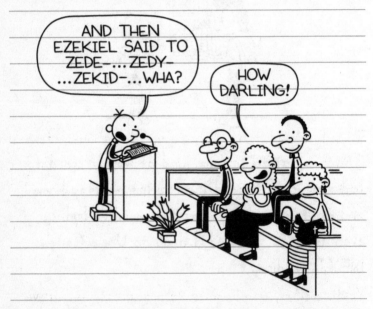

I knew Mum wasn't gonna change her mind, so I didn't spend a lot of time trying to fight it. I just went up to my room and called Rowley.

I told Rowley I couldn't go to the party so he couldn't really go, either. I explained that it wouldn't be fair for him to go while I was stuck at my uncle's wedding.

But Rowley said he's practically a grown-up now and he can make his OWN decisions, so he's going to the party no matter what.

I got so mad that I hung up the phone. Now do you see what I mean about Rowley? That's just the kind of selfish move that makes me glad we aren't friends anymore.

Saturday
Yesterday my family piled into the car and drove down to Gammie's for Uncle Gary's wedding. I was in a really bad mood because of the whole party thing, and because of something else, too.

I remembered that I'm supposed to get 'the Talk' from Gammie this weekend, and I am seriously not in the mood for a lecture right now.

The last lecture I got was from Dad's brother Uncle Joe, who told me that since I'm in middle school I need to start thinking about my 'future.'

Uncle Joe drew up a chart that showed me everything I need to do between now and the end of high school to increase my chances of getting into a good university and landing a job after that. So basically Dad and Uncle Joe have the next ten years of my life planned out for me.

Anyway, I was thinking about all this, but then something happened that snapped me out of my bad mood.

Mum called Gammie to tell her we were running a little late because we had to stop to pick up my tuxedo.

THAT got my attention. I've never had to wear a tuxedo for any of Uncle Gary's other weddings, and that could only mean one thing: I'm one of the GROOMSMEN.

The night before the wedding, the groomsmen throw the guy who's getting married a really wild party. I've seen enough cable TV to know that's something I definitely want to be a part of.

I actually felt a little bad for Rodrick, because that meant he got passed over. But I figure I could take some pictures of the party so he could see everything he missed.

Mostly, though, I felt happy, because while Rowley's at some lame middle school party, I'm gonna be riding in a limo and having the time of my life. So we'll see who's a 'man' after this weekend.

And as a bonus, at the wedding I'll be paired up with one of the bridesmaids. I'm just crossing my fingers that Sonja has some cute friends.

On the way to Gammie's house, Mum made me promise that I wouldn't wipe away my relatives' kisses, because she says it's 'rude.'

But I can't really help it. When some aunt or cousin gives me a wet kiss on my cheek, I start thinking about the bacteria multiplying on my face, and I get all twitchy. The last time we went to Gammie's, I brought some of those antibacterial wipes with me to take care of the problem.

WIPE
WIPE

But I promised Mum I wouldn't wipe any kisses this time around. And I shouldn't have even done that, because the first person to greet us was Aunt Dorothy, who always kisses me full on the lips.

As soon as I was out of Mum's sight, though, I went straight for the first thing I could find to wipe my face.

Most of the family was already at Gammie's house by the time we got there. It would take me forever to describe every single person who was there, so I'll just stick with the highlights.

My cousin Benjy was there with his parents, Aunt Patricia and Uncle Tony. The last time I saw Benjy, he could only say two things —

Benjy can speak in full sentences now, and his parents say he's reading chapter books. But I wouldn't be bragging if my son could read and still wasn't potty trained.

Great Uncle Arthur was in the den, sitting in the recliner in front of the TV. I don't think I've ever had an actual conversation with Great Uncle Arthur, because all he does is grunt and make these random sounds. He stayed with us one Thanksgiving weekend, and it was like that the whole time.

MUUURP.

I can't tell if he's trying to communicate or what, but every once in a while I respond, just in case.

Great Aunt Reba was there, too, which kind of surprised me.

A few years ago Gammie invited everyone to her house on Christmas, but she accidentally forgot to send an invitation to Great Aunt Reba. She showed up anyway, but she refused to take off her coat, and she just sat there in the living room, making us all feel guilty.

Dad's second cousin Terrence was there, and the only reason I mention him is because everyone always says I look EXACTLY like he did when he was my age, which is really depressing.

In fact, when I first heard that, I looked through Gammie's photo album to see if it was true. And unfortunately, it was.

So I guess I'd better start saving up my money for plastic surgery.

Dad's cousin Byron was there, and I wasn't too excited to see him, either. At the last family reunion, Gammie sent Byron out to get milk and I rode with him. But he hit a pothole and got a flat tyre about half a kilometre from the house.

Byron told me to go to the house and get help, and on my way back it started raining. When I walked through the front door, all the ladies in the kitchen started yelling at me for tracking mud on the floor.

They told me to take my shoes off and put them in the mudroom, which I did. But all that yelling must've rattled me, because I forgot all about Byron's flat tyre. And when he came back to the house half an hour later, he wasn't too happy.

Uncle Charlie was there, and I was really glad to see him because he's always got his pockets stuffed with lollies for us kids.

But I didn't always like Uncle Charlie, because he used to tease me when I was little. I used to have this pair of red footie pyjamas, and every time Uncle Charlie saw me, he'd say the same thing—

HEY THERE, RED!

For some reason it really got under my skin. I told Mum how I felt, and she took me to the store to get some new pyjamas, which were blue. So the next time I saw Uncle Charlie, I knew I had him beat.

But it only took him about three seconds to give me a NEW nickname.

The only person who DIDN'T show up to Gammie's was Uncle Lawrence, but that wasn't really a big surprise. Uncle Lawrence is always travelling, and he almost never comes to family gatherings. But sometimes he makes an appearance by webcam, like he did at Great Grandpa Chester's funeral.

The last people to arrive were Uncle Gary and his fiancée, Sonja. She seemed nice enough, and I guess they're pretty crazy about each other from the way they were acting.

Unfortunately, I had to sit right next to them at the dinner table and find out firsthand.

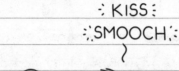

Dad told us on the way down that Sonja was kind of sensitive about the fact that Uncle Gary was married before, so we shouldn't bring it up.

Apparently, Sonja told Uncle Gary that he was gonna have to get the tattoo on his left arm removed because it had his last wife's name on it.

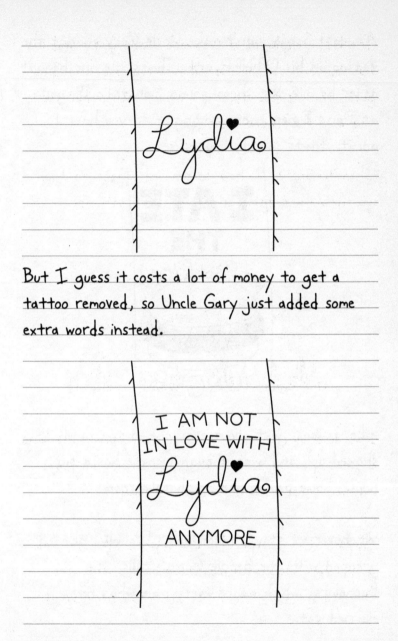

Lydia ♥

But I guess it costs a lot of money to get a tattoo removed, so Uncle Gary just added some extra words instead.

I AM NOT
IN LOVE WITH
Lydia ♥
ANYMORE

At least Sonja didn't make Uncle Gary change the tattoo on his OTHER arm. That's the one he got after he ate the three-pound Monstrilla Burger at Dan's Diner in one sitting. And you have to admit, that's pretty impressive.

Like I said, just about everyone in the family showed up, and even though Gammie has a big house, some people had to share a room.

Whenever we stay at Gammie's, I always get grouped with the people Gammie calls 'the Bachelors', which means every male who's not married yet.

THE BACHELORS

This is not a group I'm real eager to share a room with, ESPECIALLY since there are only two beds in Gammie's guest room. That means some of us have to double up and the rest have to sleep on the floor.

MAN, YOUR FEET ARE COLD!

Uncle John used to be one of the Bachelors, but he got married last spring. I'm starting to wonder if maybe he got married just so he wouldn't have to sleep in there with the rest of us.

It was hard falling asleep with all those people snoring away in the same room with me, so eventually I picked up my stuff and looked for somewhere else to spend the night.

The only place I could find was the bathroom next to Gammie's room, so I put my blanket and pillow in the tub and made myself a bed. It wasn't comfortable, but at least I had some privacy.

Luckily, when Gammie came in this morning for her bath, I woke up in the nick of time.

After that near disaster, I was up for the day. And it was a really long day, too, because the rehearsal dinner wasn't until 7:00 at night.

But at least I knew I had the party with the groomsmen to look forward to after that.

The problem with these family gatherings is that they're not really geared towards kids. So if you don't like to drink tea and gossip with the ladies, you're sort of out of luck.

And everything in Gammie's house is old-person stuff, so there's nothing for a kid to entertain himself with. I complained to Mum a few years ago, and she bought some Legos to keep at Gammie's house. But Gammie glued them together in one big block because she didn't like the little pieces all over the place.

Besides that, there's not a whole lot for a kid to enjoy at Gammie's. She DOES have some hard lollies in a jar on her mantel, and last year I had a few pieces. But the lollies tasted AWFUL. They were really chewy, like bubble gum.

I ended up getting really sick and had to lie down on the couch for a few hours.

It turns out the lollies in that jar are REALLY old.

In fact, Dad said those same lollies were there when HE was a little kid. And he even found a picture in Gammie's photo album to prove it.

Little Frankie
enjoys a sweet

Speaking of pictures, Gammie really needs to update the ones she's got on her mantel. She has a photo of every single person in the family, and the one of me and Rodrick is from when we went to Santa's Village about eight years ago.

I keep meaning to throw that picture away when no one's looking, because that's just the kind of thing that'll crop up when they do my celebrity biography later on.

🎄 Season's Greetings

All the furniture in Gammie's house is old, too, and apparently it's really valuable. I'm sure there's gonna be a big fight over who gets what once Gammie passes away. In fact, people have already started putting sticky notes on the furniture to get a head start.

I think that's pretty disrespectful to Gammie.
But I admit there are one or two items I'm
hoping to snag for myself.

<u>Sunday</u>
During the wedding rehearsal last night, I kept
thinking Uncle Gary was gonna take me aside and
tell me where the bachelor party was gonna be,
but it didn't happen.

Then I looked at the wedding program and saw
my name at the bottom.

Ring Bearer/Flower Boy .... Manny Heffley

Assistant Flower Boy .... Greg Heffley

Please, no flash photography in the church.

I tried to get out of it and turn my assistant flower boy duties over to Benjy, but Mum said he was a reader this year, and besides, me and Manny had matching white tuxedos.

So while Rowley was having a blast at Jordan Jury's party, I was holding a basket filled with rose petals for Manny. And I noticed Rodrick was taking a bunch of pictures, so I'd be surprised if he hasn't already uploaded them by now.

After the wedding ceremony, we went into the hall where the food was being served.

But before we started eating, Uncle Gary's best man, Leonard, stood up and gave a toast.

Leonard said he had a really funny story about Uncle Gary and Sonja from when they were dating and he wanted to share it with everyone. He said that a couple of months ago, Uncle Gary took Sonja to a baseball game, and he was planning on breaking up with her because he wanted to start dating her sister instead.

But before Uncle Gary could have the breakup talk with Sonja, a plane flew across the sky with a banner behind it.

Leonard said there must've been some OTHER guy in the stadium with a girlfriend named Sonja. But Uncle Gary's Sonja reacted before he had a chance to say anything.

Leonard said Uncle Gary wanted to explain that it was all just a misunderstanding, but he was too afraid that the guys in the seats around them might beat him up if he let Sonja down. So Uncle Gary decided to go along with it. At first I thought Leonard's story was just a joke, but Uncle Gary wasn't exactly jumping out of his chair to say it wasn't true.

Anyway, I have a feeling we'll be back next year for Uncle Gary's FIFTH wedding.

After the reception, our family went back to Gammie's house to get changed. I was gathering up my stuff when Dad walked into the room and said Gammie wanted to talk to me. At first I couldn't figure out why Gammie wanted to speak to me in private, but then I realised I was about to get 'the Talk.'

When I walked down the hallway to Gammie's sitting room, I was a little nervous, but I was also kind of excited. Gammie's been around the block about a million times, and I figured she's got a lot of wisdom stored up. And to be honest with you, these days I could really use some.

I walked in and shut the door behind me. Gammie was sitting in a fancy chair, so I sat across from her. Once I got settled, Gammie started talking.

Gammie told me that most kids my age are in a big rush to grow up but that if I was smart, I'd enjoy the ride while it lasts.

Now, I've heard this same speech from Mum and Dad about a billion times, so I was kind of disappointed by where this was all heading.

But Gammie wasn't finished. She said I was getting ready to enter 'the Awkward Years' and that my lips were gonna get all puffy and my skin was gonna get bad and my head was gonna look too big for my body until my junior or senior year of high school.

Then she said I shouldn't let anyone take my picture for the next few years, because I'd regret it if I did. She told me she gave the same advice to people like Dad and Uncle Gary and Uncle Joe, but they didn't listen to her.

UNCLE GARY   UNCLE JOE   DAD

But Gammie STILL wasn't done. She told me that getting older is no walk in the park and that getting to be her age REALLY stinks.

Then she started talking about 'haemorrhoids' and 'shingles' and a bunch of other stuff I'd never heard of before. I guess she could tell I was confused, so she started rolling down a sock to show me what she was talking about.

That's when I excused myself and quickly left the room. I'm glad I got out of there before Gammie decided to take off any more clothes.

A half hour later we packed up our things, got in the car, and headed home. I was just happy the weekend was over. I love my relatives and all, but there's only so much family togetherness I can take.

HEY! POOPY DIAPER HERE!

<u>Monday</u>
It was a drag going back to school today, because it seemed like everyone went to Jordan Jury's party, and of course that was all anyone wanted to talk about.

Walking through the older kids' hallway was the WORST.

I'm actually kind of glad I didn't go. I found out the reason Jordan invited kids in my grade was to basically use them as servants.

Tonight on the news they announced the winner of the Peachy Breeze Kid contest, and unfortunately I didn't get picked. But I do know the kid who DID.

It was Scotty Douglas, who lives right down the street. Don't ask me why they picked him, because he couldn't even get the slogan right in the audition.

But the people at Peachy Breeze should've done their research, because if they saw Scotty's older brother, they might've thought twice.

Last night Mum said now that her first semester of school is over, she's going to put her academic career 'on hold' for a while and spend more time with the family. I can't tell you how happy I was to hear that. I'm glad things will finally be getting back to normal around here.

In fact, that's been the whole problem this year. There's been a lot of change all of a sudden, and I really liked things the way they were BEFORE.

People like Dad and Uncle Joe have been getting on my case to act more responsible and start getting serious about my future. But the truth is, I think I'm more of an Uncle Gary kind of guy.

I guess I'm just not in a big rush to grow up right now. And after Gammie showed me what's in store over the next few years, I think I'm gonna take her advice and hang on as long as I can.

Tuesday
Speaking of things getting back to normal, I decided it was time for me and Rowley to put the past couple of months behind us and get our friendship back on track.

Me and him have a really long history together, and there's no point in throwing that away over something dumb.

And to be honest with you, I can't even remember what we were fighting about.

So after school today I went up to Rowley's house to see if he wanted to hang out. He was so happy to see me that it was kind of embarrassing.

Rowley asked me if we'd be 'best friends forever,' and he gave me half of this matching locket he's always tried to get me to wear.

I told him I wasn't gonna wear the locket, because it's meant for girls. But really, it's that 'forever' word that makes me nervous. I told him maybe we could just take it one month at a time, and he seemed pretty satisfied with that.

I'll say one thing, though. Rowley must've grown a full inch and a half since the summer, so who KNOWS how tall this kid is gonna be.

I figure it's a good idea for me to stick with him, at least until we get to high school. Because if he keeps growing at this rate, Rowley's gonna be a good person to have at my side.

ACKNOWLEDGMENTS

Thanks to all the fans of the *Wimpy Kid* series for making my dream of being a cartoonist come true.

Thanks to my family for the continued love and support. This wouldn't be much fun if I couldn't share it with you. Thanks to Mum and Dad for the incredible support you give to me and to all your kids.

Thanks to the folks at Abrams for putting so much care and attention to detail into these books. A special thanks to Charlie Kochman, my editor; Jason Wells, my publicist; Chad W. Beckerman, art director; and Scott Auerbach, managing editor. Thanks to Michael Jacobs for believing a Wimpy Kid could fly.

Thanks to Patrick for being a great sounding board and helping up the comic ante. Thanks to Jess for your friendship and mentorship. Thanks to Shaelyn for your tireless assistance in improving this book.

Thanks to everyone in Hollywood for working so hard to bring the world of *Wimpy Kid* to life, especially Nina, Brad, Carla, Riley, Elizabeth, Nick, Thor, and David. And thanks, Sylvie and Keith, for your help and guidance.

ABOUT THE AUTHOR

Jeff Kinney is an online game developer and designer, and a #1 *New York Times* bestselling author. In 2009, Jeff was named one of *Time* magazine's 100 Most Influential People in the World. Jeff is also the creator of Poptropica.com. He spent his childhood in the Washington, D.C., area and moved to New England in 1995. Jeff lives in southern Massachusetts with his wife and their two sons.

ALSO BY JEFF KINNEY

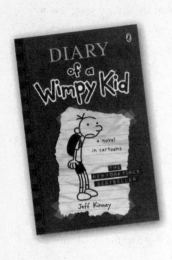

Being a kid can really stink. And no one knows this better than Greg Heffley, who finds himself thrust into high school, where undersized weaklings share the hallways with kids who are taller, meaner, and already shaving.

Luckily Greg has his best friend and sidekick, Rowley. But when Rowley's popularity starts to rise, it kicks off a chain of events that will test their friendship in hilarious fashion.

Whatever you do, don't ask Greg Heffley how he spent his summer vacation, because he definitely doesn't want to talk about it.

As Greg enters the new school year, he's eager to put the events of the past three months behind him . . . one event in particular he wants to keep secret.

Unfortunately for him, his older brother, Rodrick, knows all about it. And secrets have a way of getting out . . . especially when a diary is involved.

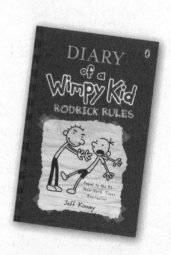

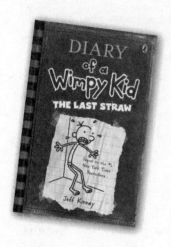

Let's face it: Greg Heffley will never change his wimpy ways. Somebody just needs to explain that to Greg's father.

You see, Frank Heffley actually thinks he can get his son to toughen up, and he enlists Greg in organised sports and other 'manly' endeavours.

Of course, Greg is easily able to sidestep his father's efforts to change him. But when Greg's dad threatens to send him to military academy, Greg realises he has to shape up . . . to get shipped out.

Greg, a self-confessed 'indoor person', is living out his ultimate summer fantasy: no responsibilities and no rules. But Greg's mum has a different vision for an ideal summer . . . one packed with outdoor activities and 'family togetherness'.

Whose vision will win out? Or will a new addition to the Heffley family change everything?

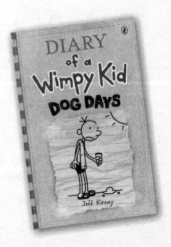

ALSO BY JEFF KINNEY

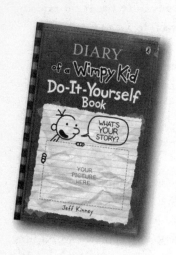

Packed with original art and all-new material, this Do-It-Yourself Book features ruled pages and empty word balloons so you can create your own stories and comics, list you favourites and least faves and keep your own daily journal. But whatever you do, make sure you put this book someplace safe after you finish it, because when you're rich and famous, this thing is going to be worth a fortune!

Ever wondered how they make a movie out of a book? Author Jeff Kinney didn't know either, but discovering how Greg Heffley and everyone else from his bestselling series, Diary of a Wimpy Kid, got turned into a live-action movie by 20th Century Fox, was an adventure he definitely wanted to share with you; so here it is!

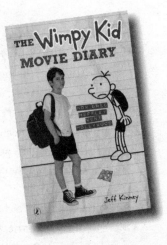